The Adventures of Lulu

Also by Louise Hay

BOOKS/KIT

All Is Well (with Mona Lisa Schulz, M.D., Ph.D.)
Colors & Numbers
Empowering Women
Everyday Positive Thinking
Experience Your Good Now!
A Garden of Thoughts: My Affirmation Journal
Gratitude: A Way of Life (Louise & Friends)
Heal Your Body
Heal Your Body A–Z
Heart Thoughts (also available in a gift edition)
I Can Do It® (book-with-CD)
Inner Wisdom
Letters to Louise
Life! Reflections on Your Journey
Love Your Body
Love Yourself, Heal Your Life Workbook
Loving Yourself to Great Health (with Ahlea Khadro and Heather Dane)
Meditations to Heal Your Life (also available
in a gift edition)
Modern-Day Miracles (Louise & Friends)
The Power Is Within You
Power Thoughts
The Present Moment
The Times of Our Lives (Louise & Friends)
You Can Create an Exceptional Life (with Cheryl Richardson)
You Can Heal Your Heart (with David Kessler)
You Can Heal Your Life (also available in a gift edition)
You Can Heal Your Life Affirmation Kit
You Can Heal Your Life Companion Book

FOR CHILDREN

The Adventures of Lulu
I Think, I Am! (with Kristina Tracy)
Lulu and the Ant: A Message of Love
Lulu and the Dark: Conquering Fears
Lulu and Willy the Duck: Learning Mirror Work

CD PROGRAMS

All Is Well (audio book)
Anger Releasing
Cancer
Change and Transition
Dissolving Barriers
Embracing Change
The Empowering Women Gift Collection
Feeling Fine Affirmations
Forgiveness/Loving the Inner Child
How to Love Yourself
Meditations for Loving Yourself to Great Health (with Ahlea Khadro and Heather Dane)
Meditations for Personal Healing
Meditations to Heal Your Life (audio book)

Morning and Evening Meditations
101 Power Thoughts
Overcoming Fears
The Power Is Within You (audio book)
The Power of Your Spoken Word
Receiving Prosperity
Self-Esteem Affirmations (subliminal)
Self-Healing
Stress-Free (subliminal)
Totality of Possibilities
What I Believe and Deep Relaxation
You Can Heal Your Life (audio book)
You Can Heal Your Life Study Course
Your Thoughts Create Your Life

DVDs

Receiving Prosperity
You Can Heal Your Life Study Course
You Can Heal Your Life, The Movie (also available in an expanded edition)
You Can Trust Your Life (with Cheryl Richardson)

CARD DECKS

Healthy Body Cards
I Can Do It® Cards
I Can Do It® Cards . . . for Creativity, Forgiveness, Health, Job Success, Wealth, Romance
Power Thought Cards
Power Thoughts for Teens
Power Thought Sticky Cards
Wisdom Cards

CALENDAR

I Can Do It® Calendar (for each individual year)

and

THE ESSENTIAL LOUISE HAY COLLECTION

(comprising You Can Heal Your Life, Heal Your Body, and The Power Is Within You in a single volume)

All of the above are available at your local bookstore, or may be ordered by visiting
Hay House USA: **www.hayhouse.com**®
Hay House Australia: **www.hayhouse.com.au**
Hay House UK: **www.hayhouse.co.uk**
Hay House South Africa: **www.hayhouse.co.za**
Hay House India: **www.hayhouse.co.in**

Websites: **www.LouiseHay.com**® and **www.HealYourLife.com**®

The Adventures of Lulu

Louise Hay
and Dan Olmos

Drawings by J. J. Smith-Moore

HAY HOUSE, INC.
Carlsbad, California • New York City
London • Sydney • Johannesburg
Vancouver • Hong Kong • New Delhi

Published and distributed in the United States by: Hay House, Inc.: www.hayhouse.com •
Published and distributed in Australia by: Hay House Australia Pty. Ltd.: www.hayhouse.com
.au • *Published and distributed in the United Kingdom by:* Hay House UK, Ltd.: www.hayhouse
.co.uk • *Published and distributed in the Republic of South Africa by:* Hay House SA (Pty),
Ltd.: www.hayhouse.co.za • *Distributed in Canada by:* Raincoast Books: www.raincoast.com •
Published in India by: Hay House Publishers India: www.hayhouse.co.in

Editorial supervision: Jill Kramer • *Design:* Amy Gingery

Library of Congress Control No.: 2004111267

ISBN 13: 978-1-4019-0553-8
ISBN 10: 1-4019-0553-6

14 13 12 11 10 9 8 7 6 5
1st printing, July 2005

Printed in the United States of America

Contents

InTroduction

We just received a letter from an adult woman telling us how helpful these books were to her as a child. They put her on the pathway to developing feelings of self-esteem and self-worth. Of course, that was exactly where I was coming from when I created the Lulu coloring books many years ago. The Lulu in the stories was the little girl I wanted to be as a child: long blonde hair, self-assured, confident, helpful to others, and willing to learn.

Dan Olmos, artist J. J. Smith-Moore, and musician Randall Leonard helped me create the original Lulu series—*Lulu and the Ant, Lulu and Willy the Duck,* and *Lulu and the Dark*—to empower children. I even narrated these stories on a 12-minute audiocassette when the coloring books were first published.

Now, Hay House is reissuing these three charming little stories as one wonderful, illustrated children's book for you and your family to enjoy. Read these stories together anytime (they're very good when read before bedtime). I hope the messages of trust, self-confidence, and love will inspire not only your children, but *you* as well.

We are all children of the Universe at any age, so enjoy!

I love you, *Louise Hay*

Part I

Lulu and the Ant:
A Message of Love

Once, not long ago, in a town not much different from yours, there lived a little girl named Lulu. She had big blue eyes and curly blonde hair, which she liked to tie with a ribbon into the tiniest little ponytail on the back of her head.

She lived in a big house with two windows on each side of the front door that made it look like a happy face, with the steps leading to the porch as the smile. There were many old trees in the yard. They protected the house and gave Lulu branches to climb on and supported an old tire to swing on. There was always something fun to do in Lulu's yard.

Many times Lulu had to play by herself. She had a baby brother whose name was Barry, and he was so small that her parents were always taking care of him. Lulu didn't mind, really. She knew that someday Barry would be older and not need so much attention.

Right now, he was just a baby and needed to be taken care of by her parents. Besides, she enjoyed playing by herself. There were so many interesting things to discover.

On one lazy afternoon, Lulu lay in the front yard and watched the clouds drift by. She made a game of imagining that the clouds were actually a circus going by.

She could see elephants and tigers and clowns,
and even a beautiful woman on a flying trapeze.

She was having the most wonderful time, when suddenly she felt something crawling on her arm. She looked down and there was an ant.

Lulu smiled and said, "Oh, it's just a little ant."

When the ant heard this, he became angry and crossed his tiny little arms across his chest and snapped, "Pffff! Well, *you're* just a little girl!"

Lulu felt sorry for what she'd said and apologized. "I'm sorry, little ant. I didn't mean it to sound like that. I'm sure that you're a very important ant."

"Oh, that's all right," he replied. "People always think we're all the same. I just get a little tired of hearing it.

Whenever we go to people's picnics or are wandering through their homes, we always hear the same thing: 'Ants!' People don't realize that we're all different, just like you are."

Lulu liked the little ant. She leaned down closer and said, "You're a nice little ant. Tell me some more."

The little ant was so happy to talk with a new friend. "We're building a city under the ground called CincinnANTi," he told her.

"I have a big rock to move, only you're in my way. I was gonna tickle your ear so that you might move."

Lulu got up quickly and offered, "I can help you move the rock. I'm very strong."

The little ant was so pleased. He quickly crawled back to where he had left his rock and said, "Here it is! Can you lift this?"

The rock was very, very small to Lulu. In fact, it was more like a large grain of sand. She carefully pinched the rock between her fingers and moved it to where he wanted it. The ant was so happy.

"You would make a wonderful ant," he said. "Won't you come and live with me? Why, with you working with us, we'd have our city built in no time!"

Lulu smiled at the ant. "I'm afraid I wouldn't fit in your city. It's so much smaller than I am. I just couldn't be an ant."

The little ant looked puzzled. "But why can't you?" he asked. "In my city we have a little song that we sing all the time. It goes like this:

You can be what you want to be, you can do what you want to do, you can be what you want to be, all of life supports you."

"That's a funny little song," Lulu giggled, "but what does it mean?"

"It means that we may all be different, but we each have the power within us to do wonderful things with our lives," the little ant explained. "You can do what you want to do. There's nothing to stop you."

"I like to dance," Lulu said. "I'd love to be a ballerina."

"You can if you want," the little ant told her.

Lulu looked down at her new friend and said sadly, "I don't think so. My mother took me to a dance class, and the teacher said that my legs were too skinny and that I wouldn't make a good ballerina."

The little ant stomped his tiny foot as loud as a little ant can stomp it. "If you want to be a ballerina, you can be a ballerina!" he shouted. "Let me show you a little trick. It starts in your mind."

Lulu sat straight up and listened carefully to what the little ant said.

"We're going to play a game. Begin by imagining yourself in the most beautiful theater in the world."

Lulu shut her eyes and suddenly in front of her she could see herself in the most beautiful theater she could imagine.

"Now," the little ant continued, "see yourself dancing onstage. You're the prettiest and most graceful ballerina there ever was. Can you see it?"

Lulu *could* see it. She was so excited that she almost opened her eyes, but she wanted the feeling to last forever. There she was on the stage, dancing beautifully—even if her legs were still a little skinny. Slowly, her vision faded and she opened her eyes. "I saw it!" she cried. "I was so beautiful and dancing so gracefully! Oh, thank you! I just know that I can become a wonderful ballerina if I want to!" And then she frowned.

"But I also like horses," Lulu said. "Could I become a horseback rider in the circus?"

"Of course you can," her tiny pal replied. "If that's what you truly want, then you'll find a way to get it. Just play this imagination game."

Lulu closed her eyes and imagined herself standing atop a majestic white horse as it galloped around the ring of the circus. She felt so happy. But then she frowned again.

"But I also like to help people when they're sick," Lulu explained. "Do you think I could become a doctor?"

"You can do that, too, if you want to," the little ant affirmed.

Lulu imagined herself working in a lovely doctor's office helping people get well. She became very excited. "There really are so many things I can do, aren't there?!" she exclaimed.

The little ant smiled a great big smile. "Of course there are. Just remember: Whenever you feel that you can't do something, imagine yourself doing it. Your thoughts are very powerful. They can make so many good things happen for you. Sometimes it takes a little while, but it will happen if you really want it. And also, sing my little song to yourself all the time. It will help remind you that nothing is impossible." And he sang once more:

"You can be what you want to be, you can do what you want to do, you can be what you want to be, all of life supports you."

"Now I have to get back to work," the little ant said.
Lulu smiled down at her new friend. "Thank you for talking to me. I really had a wonderful time. Can we talk again?"

"Of course we can," the little ant smiled. "I'd invite you to dinner, but you wouldn't fit in my house. Perhaps we can have a picnic. We ants love people picnics. You can bring the food."

"That would be fun!" Lulu agreed. And with that, the little ant scurried back into the little hole in the ground to get back to work.

It had been a lovely afternoon. The warm breeze played with Lulu's hair, then raced through the leaves in the trees. In the distance, Lulu could hear her baby brother, Barry, making the gurgly sounds that only babies know how to make.

Her mother came out to the front porch and called, "Lulu, come in now. It's time for dinner!"

Lulu got up off the ground, dusted herself off, and happily headed toward the house while singing the song that the little ant had taught her:

"I can be what I want to be, I can do what I want to do, I can be what I want to be, all of life supports me."

Part II
Lulu and Willy the Duck:
Learning Mirror Work

The sun was almost always shining on the big house with two windows on each side of the front door that made it look like a happy face (with the steps leading to the porch as the smile). Lulu loved to play outside in the yard, sometimes under the trees and sometimes on the tire swing, and sometimes with her little brother, Barry.

Lulu knew that there was always something fun to do, and she woke up each morning excited to find out what would happen that day.

On this morning, Lulu woke to the sounds of raindrops falling on the tree outside the window. She loved the rain, and as she got out of bed, she decided to show her little brother, Barry, the wet weather. He was very young and couldn't get out of his crib by himself yet.

Barry laughed as Lulu picked him up and took him to the window. He still couldn't talk very well, and when he said Lulu's name, it sounded like, "Wuwu."

"Wuwu, wawa!" Barry yelled, jumping up and down.

"It's rain, Barry," his big sister explained. "It makes the trees grow and the flowers bloom and makes everything fresh and beautiful!"

Barry laughed again.

Suddenly, Lulu heard a sound in the distance—a funny kind of sound: "Wah! Wah!" Somebody was crying. Lulu thought they might be hurt, so she lifted Barry back into his crib and went downstairs to put on her raincoat. She took her umbrella with the flowers on it and hurried out the back door to see who was crying.

As she walked across the lawn, she saw a frog sitting under a tree enjoying the rain. "Good morning, Mr. Frog," Lulu greeted him. "It's a beautiful morning, isn't it?"

"Beautiful! Wet and rainy!" agreed Mr. Frog. "It would be perfect except for that crying."

"Do you know who it is?" Lulu asked.

"No," Mr. Frog answered, "but it's coming from the pond. Why don't we hop over there together." And with that, he hopped off as Lulu followed behind him.

As they got near the pond, the cries became louder and louder: "Wah! Wah!" Lulu listened carefully and went to a patch of tall grass. Mr. Frog jumped beside her.

They both poked their heads into the grass, and sitting inside was a little yellow duck, crying his eyes out.

"Wah! Woe is me!" wailed the little duck. Lulu put her hand on the duck's head and softly stroked it.

"Why are you crying?" she asked.

The little fellow raised his head. "Oh, nobody likes me— nobody at all," he sobbed.

"No one?" asked the frog. "I'd say that's pretty serious."

Lulu continued to pet the little duck. "Well, I like you. What's your name?"

The duckling looked up and dried his eyes. "My name is Willy."

"Well, my name is Lulu, and this is Mr. Frog. Maybe we can help you," Lulu offered.

"Why do you think no one likes you?"

Willy sat up and said, "This morning I was playing ball with some of the farm animals from down the street. Gary the Goat threw the ball to me, and when I tried to catch it, I tripped over my feet and fell in the mud and lost my cap! Oh, woe is me!"

"But Willy, what's so horrible about that?" Lulu asked. "It was an accident, and you didn't hurt yourself, did you?"

"No," Willy sniffled, "but then Clarice the Calf called me 'Willy Bigfoot,' and everybody started laughing. They wouldn't stop, so I ran away, and now I have no more friends!"

Lulu petted Willy's head some more. "Oh, Willy," she exclaimed, "don't you know that the best friend you can ever have is YOU?"

"But I don't like me!" Willy cried. "I'm dumb and clumsy!"

Mr. Frog looked at Willy and laughed. "Willy, you have no idea how many times I've tripped over my own two feet. Mine are much bigger than yours. It's really not such a terrible thing. It's just how you look at it. I've seen you in the pond, and you're a very good swimmer—better than I am. That's something to be proud of."

Willy felt a little better.

"And last week I saw you rescue Baby Kitten when she fell into the pond. Mama Cat was so happy, and she thought you were so brave," Mr. Frog continued.

"She did?" Willy asked.

"You see," Lulu added, "there are many good things about you. You just haven't been looking for them. You know what I do when I'm feeling bad?"

"What?" Willy asked.

"In my room I have a mirror, and I call it my Magic Mirror. Inside this mirror is my very best friend. She's always going to be there for me, and when something goes wrong, she can make me feel better. And I can make her feel better, too."

"But I don't have a Magic Mirror," Willy said.

Lulu leaned close to the little duck. "I can take you to mine. Your best friend will be there, too."

Willy got so excited! "Oh, take me to your Magic Mirror, please!" he squealed.

"Okay," Lulu answered. "Follow me. Do you want to go, too, Mr. Frog?"

Mr. Frog took a look at the pond and said, "I think I'll stay here and go swimming. Nothing like a good swim in the morning. Gets the blood going, you know?" And with a splish-splash, he was gone.

Lulu and Willy started back toward the house. "You see, Willy," Lulu began, "what you think about yourself will come true, so you don't want to think bad things."

"You mean I'm dumb and clumsy because I think I am?" Willy asked.

"Of course," Lulu answered. "One time at school, I was running a race, and I was sure that I couldn't win it. I kept telling myself, 'Oh, Lulu, you'll never win,' and guess what happened?"

"You didn't win?" Willy guessed.

"Right! So the next time, I decided to say over
and over to myself, 'You can do it! You can do it!'
and you know what?"

"You won!" Willy shouted.

"Yes!" Lulu said. "It really made a difference."

Finally, they arrived at Lulu's house. They walked through the front door, past the kitchen, down the hall, up the stairs, and into Lulu's room. Next to her bed on the wall was the Magic Mirror.

Willy shouted with joy, "Oh, I'm going to meet my best friend! I'm going to meet my best friend!"

Lulu set a chair in front of the mirror and told Willy to shut his eyes. Willy did as he was told, and Lulu put him on the chair.

"Okay, now when you open your eyes, you'll see your best friend. This is the person who will always be with you and who will never leave you. . . . Open them now!"

Willy opened his eyes and was surprised to find that he was looking at himself. "But it's just me," he said.

"That's right," Lulu replied. "No matter what happens to you in your life, your best friend is always going to be yourself.

Say something nice to yourself."

Willy felt shy. "Hello," he ventured quietly, then turned to Lulu. "I don't know what to say."

"Tell him about the nice things that were said about you today," Lulu suggested.

"You're a good swimmer, and Mama Cat thinks you're brave," Willy said.

"That's good," Lulu encouraged him. "Can you say, 'I love you'?"

"That sounds silly," Willy replied.

"Just try it," she pleaded.

Willy looked at himself in the mirror. "Well," he began again, "I love you, and I'm sorry that I thought you were dumb and clumsy."

And you know what? Willy felt a little better.

He tried again, "I love you, I really love you," and he felt even better. The more he said it, the better he felt.

"Oh, Lulu," he cried, "I've never felt so good about myself!"

Lulu was so happy for Willy. Now he would know that no one is ever really alone as long as they have themselves.

It was getting late now, and it was time for Willy to go home.

"Oh, Lulu," Willy sighed, "I wish I could take your Magic Mirror with me."

"You don't need to have my mirror, Willy," Lulu explained. "Any mirror will do. In fact, the pond you live in is the best mirror of all."

"Thank you!" he exclaimed. "Then I can look into the pond every day and see my best friend."

"And you'll remember to say nice things to yourself?" Lulu asked. "Be sure to say, 'I love you, I really love you.'"

"Oh yes!" Willy replied. He happily sang, "Willy, I love you, I really love you!" as he and Lulu walked down the stairs, through the hall, and past the kitchen where Barry was now sitting in his high chair.

When Barry saw Willy walk by, he shouted, "Ducky!"

Lulu smiled as she heard her mother answer, "Now, Barry, there are no ducks in the house."

Outside, the rain had stopped, and the sun was shining brightly. Lulu and Willy were walking back to the pond when they found all of Willy's friends.

Gary the Goat asked, "Where have you been, Willy? Here's your cap. We're playing ball, and we need you on our team."

"I've been visiting with my best friend," Willy
answered proudly. He turned to Lulu and asked her to
bend down because he had a secret to tell her.

Lulu bent down close, and quick as a wink, Willy
gave her a kiss on the cheek. "Thank you, Lulu," he
said. "You've given me a wonderful new friend today."

"You're welcome," Lulu smiled. "But remember, you have to keep being a friend to yourself just like you would any other friend. The more you love yourself, the happier you'll be—you'll see."

And with that, Willy waved to Lulu and ran off with his friends to play ball.

Part III

Lulu and the Dark:
Conquering Fears

Lulu liked to spend time outdoors in her nice yard. There were many trees, and one of them even had a tire swing hanging from it. Lulu had such a good time there that she felt as if she were friends with all the flowers, insects, and animals.

It was lots of fun to be outside, but after a long day of playing, Lulu was happy to go indoors and spend the evening with her mother and father and her little brother, Barry.

One night, it was late and time for Lulu to go to bed. She usually didn't mind going to bed, but on this night she and Barry had watched a scary movie on television, and it had frightened her.

"Fraidy-cat, fraidy-cat!" Barry teased Lulu as he went to his room.

"I am not!" Lulu insisted.

Barry peered around the door and whispered one last time, "Fraidy-cat!"

"Lulu," her mother said. "It was just a movie. There's nothing in your room to be afraid of, but I'll tuck you in to make sure you're safe."

Lulu ran upstairs to her room to put her pajamas on. She loved her pajamas because they had circus animals all over them. She had taken the time to name each and every one of them—her favorites were the carousel horses.

As she got into bed, she thought about the scary movie she'd just watched. Oh, how she wished she hadn't seen it! She clutched her doll, Mandy, close to her. Mandy also had blue eyes and curly blonde hair, and Lulu loved Mandy very much.

Lulu's mother came into her bedroom. "Now Lulu, you're not going to be scared of the dark, are you?" she asked.

Lulu tried to be brave. "No, Mommy," she replied, not wanting to show that she was really afraid.

Lulu's mother tucked her tightly into bed. Lulu loved it when her mother tucked her in. It always made her feel safe and loved.

"Get a good night's sleep, Lulu. I love you," her mother said, and kissed her good night.

"I love you, too, Mommy," Lulu answered. Then out went the light, and her mother was gone.

Lulu lay in the darkness. She wished she could get up and turn the light back on, but she was afraid that if she put her foot on the floor, something would grab her from under the bed.

I'll just lie here very still, she thought. *Then if anything is in the room, it will never know I'm here.*

The moonlight came through the bedroom window, and Lulu could see a bit more. She felt a little better, but then she decided to just keep her eyes shut.

Suddenly, she thought she heard a noise at the foot of the bed. "Oh no," she said to Mandy, "a monster!" She kept her eyes shut tight, but finally couldn't stand it any longer. She opened her eyes and sat up, and there at the end of the bed was a witch wearing a big black hat pulled over her hair. Lulu was so scared!

"What do you want?" Lulu asked in a small voice. But the witch said nothing.

"Please go away!" Lulu said, but still the witch said nothing.

Lulu couldn't stand it anymore. "Mommy! Daddy!" she cried out as she pulled the covers over her head.

Lulu's mother and father quickly came into the room. "What's wrong?" they both asked at once. Barry stood quietly in the doorway.

Still under the covers, Lulu yelled, "There's a witch at the foot of my bed!"

Both her parents started laughing. "Lulu, take a look at your witch," they chuckled.

She peeked out from under the covers and saw her chair at the end of the bed with a blouse hanging on it. Lulu was so embarrassed! There was nothing to be afraid of after all.

"Now, Lulu," her father said, "the next time you're scared, close your eyes and think of the most wonderful place you can be. It will help you not be afraid anymore. When I was afraid of the dark, I used to imagine that I was a ship's captain on the high seas, and I would soon forget that I was scared."

He gave Lulu a kiss on her forehead, and her mother brought her a glass of water and put it on the nightstand.

Barry just stood by the door and snickered. "Fraidy-cat," he whispered just before he went back to his own room.

Lulu's parents kissed her good night once more and returned to their room. Lulu lay in the dark once more. Outside, the tree branches brushed against the window. "Mandy," Lulu said, "let's make believe that we're somewhere else and maybe we won't be so afraid, just like Daddy said."

Lulu shut her eyes and told Mandy to shut hers, too. Then Lulu pretended that she was playing in a field of the most beautiful flowers she'd ever seen. Mandy was there, too, only she was just as big as Lulu.

"Oh, Lulu," Mandy exclaimed, "this is such a wonderful place! I wish we could stay here forever."

Lulu loved it in the field, too. The sun was shining, the flowers smelled so sweet, and the birds were singing happily in the trees. One bird was a kindly owl who wore a baseball cap. He flew down and sat on an old tree stump near Lulu and Mandy.

"Whooo! Whooo! Who are you?" the owl asked.

"I'm Lulu, and this is my friend Mandy," Lulu answered.

"Glad to meet you," the owl said. "We don't get many visitors here."

Lulu told him how she and Mandy were frightened of the dark, and this was a much nicer place to be.

"Well," the owl replied, "people are most afraid of the things they don't understand. Take the dark, for instance. The dark is really very nice—you just have to become its friend."

"How do you do that?" Mandy asked.

"By learning about it," the owl explained. "Let's take a walk to the waterfall, and I'll tell you more."

So Lulu and Mandy started walking toward the waterfall. The owl sat on Lulu's shoulder pointing the way. The waterfall was even *more* beautiful than Lulu or Mandy could imagine. There were green plants everywhere, and in the water, fish jumped and played so happily.

"You see," the owl told them, "the dark is important to us because it gives everything a chance to rest. Everything needs rest—the birds, animals, plants, and even those fish in the stream. Just think how tired they'd be if they never got any sleep."

"But sometimes the dark is scary," Lulu argued. "Last night I was trying to go to sleep, but I kept hearing creaking noises in my room like somebody was walking across the floor."

The owl laughed. "Ho-ho! That used to scare me when I was little, too.

My grandmother was a very wise old owl, and she told me that those noises were just the house getting ready for bed. Your house stands so straight and tall all day long, and at night it likes to take a rest, too. *You* try to get into bed without making any sound at all. I bet you can't do it."

Lulu and Mandy laughed—they liked the owl. He made them feel much better because he was kind and patient with them and didn't think they were silly at all for being afraid of the dark.

"My grandmother also taught me a little song," he continued. "Whenever I was feeling afraid of the dark, I'd sing it over and over to myself. Do you want to hear it?"

"Oh yes!" Lulu and Mandy said together.

The owl straightened up and proudly sang:

"There's nothing here for me to fear. I'm safe and well protected."

"That's a lovely song," Lulu said. "I'll sing it the next time I'm afraid."

"Me, too," Mandy agreed.

The owl was so happy that they liked his song.

Then they all noticed that the sun was starting to set. "Well, it's time for me to go," the owl said. "I'm going to an Owl Scout campfire meeting. That's another nice thing about the dark: Campfires always look better in the dark. So do the moon, the stars, and drive-in movies."

Lulu and Mandy smiled at the owl. "Thank you so much for talking to us. We've learned so much."

"You're welcome," he replied. "Just remember my little song and know that nothing will ever frighten you again." And with that he flew away singing his little song:

"There's nothing here for me to fear. I'm safe and well protected."

Lulu and Mandy stayed to watch the sunset, and soon the moon smiled down at them. The stars came out and sparkled brightly . . . and suddenly it was morning.

Lulu woke up in her bed with Mandy next to her on the pillow.

What a wonderful dream! Lulu thought. *Now I don't have to be afraid of anything.*

Just then her door opened, and a ghost walked in—only this ghost was wearing slippers with clowns' heads on them, just like Barry's.

"Boooo!" the ghost moaned, and then out popped Barry, laughing. Lulu giggled, too.

Barry could be a pest, but he was also a lot of fun. Lulu told him about her wonderful dream and the song she'd learned.

"Oh, please teach it to me," Barry begged. "You know that sometimes I get afraid, too."

Lulu hugged Mandy tightly as she taught Barry the owl's song. Holding hands, they raced downstairs to eat breakfast, still singing their special song:

"There's nothing here for me to fear. I'm safe and well protected.

"There's nothing here for me to fear. I'm safe and well protected."

About Louise Hay

Louise Hay is a metaphysical lecturer and teacher and the best-selling author of numerous books, including *You Can Heal Your Life* and *I Can Do It*®. Her works have been translated into 29 different languages in 35 countries throughout the world. For more than 30 years, Louise has assisted millions of people in discovering and using the full potential of their own creative powers for personal growth and self-healing. Louise is the founder of Hay House, Inc., a publishing company that disseminates books, audios, and videos that contribute to the healing of the planet. Websites: **www.LouiseHay.com**® and **www.HealYourLife.com**®

Hay House Titles of Related Interest

Books

BABY SIGN LANGUAGE BASICS: Early Communication for Hearing Babies and Toddlers, by Monta Z. Briant

THE CARE AND FEEDING OF INDIGO CHILDREN, by Doreen Virtue

THE CRYSTAL CHILDREN, by Doreen Virtue

THE INDIGO CHILDREN: The New Kids Have Arrived, by Lee Carroll and Jan Tober

THE JOURNEY HOME: Children's Edition, by Theresa Corley

PARENTS' NUTRITION BIBLE, by Earl Mindell, R.Ph., Ph.D.

SEVEN SECRETS TO RAISING A HAPPY AND HEALTHY CHILD, by Joyce Golden Seyburn

Card Decks

CAR GO CARDS: Fabulously Foolproof on-the-Road Activities for Fidgety Kids, from the Publishers of *Parenting* magazine

RAINY-DAY FUN CARDS: Easy Indoor Games and Activities Your Kids Will Love, from the Publishers of *Parenting* magazine

SIGN LANGUAGE FOR BABIES CARDS: 50 Easy Words to Learn—from Sleep to I Love You, from the Publishers of *Parenting* magazine

All of the above are available at your local bookstore, or may be ordered by visiting Hay House (see next page for contact info).

♡ ⚭ ♡ ⚭ ♡

We hope you enjoyed this Hay House book. If you'd like to receive our online catalog featuring additional information on Hay House books and products, or if you'd like to find out more about the Hay Foundation, please contact:

Hay House, Inc.
P.O. Box 5100
Carlsbad, CA 92018-5100

(760) 431-7695 or **(800) 654-5126**
(760) 431-6948 (fax) or **(800) 650-5115 (fax)**
www.hayhouse.com® • **www.hayfoundation.org**

♥

Published and distributed in Australia by: Hay House Australia Pty. Ltd., 18/36 Ralph St., Alexandria NSW 2015 • *Phone:* 612-9669-4299 • *Fax:* 612-9669-4144 • www.hayhouse.com.au

Published and distributed in the United Kingdom by: Hay House UK, Ltd., Astley House, 33 Notting Hill Gate, London W11 3JQ • *Phone:* 44-20-3675-2450 • *Fax:* 44-20-3675-2451 www.hayhouse.co.uk

Published and distributed in the Republic of South Africa by: Hay House SA (Pty), Ltd., P.O. Box 990, Witkoppen 2068 • info@hayhouse.co.za • www.hayhouse.co.za

Published in India by: Hay House Publishers India, Muskaan Complex, Plot No. 3, B-2, Vasant Kunj, New Delhi 110 070 • *Phone:* 91-11-4176-1620 • *Fax:* 91-11-4176-1630 • www.hayhouse.co.in

Distributed in Canada by: Raincoast Books, 2440 Viking Way, Richmond, B.C. V6V 1N2 *Phone:* 1-800-663-5714 • *Fax:* 1-800-565-3770 • www.raincoast.com

Take Your Soul on a Vacation

Visit **www.HealYourLife.com**® to regroup, recharge, and reconnect with your own magnificence. Featuring blogs, mind-body-spirit news, and life-changing wisdom from Louise Hay and friends.

Visit **www.HealYourLife.com** today!